The Train To Christmas Town

Story by Peggy Ellis

Illustrated by Jeffrey Lee

ABOUT THE AUTHOR

Peggy Bullard Ellis is an elementary special education
teacher who has written for Trains Magazine and rides
trains year round. Her three children grew up with
trains and were wonderful inspirations for this book.
Find her at peggybullardellis.wordpress.com

ABOUT THE ILLUSTRATOR

Jeffrey Lee is best known for designing Q*Bert
& his foes in the classic arcade game. You can
see his artwork at http://qbertlee.blogspot.com/
or buy his book "How The Turtle Got Its Shell" at
http://www.amazon.com/How-The-Turtle-Shell-ebook/dp/B007VCSEYY

J anice loved riding the train to Christmas Town. Every December her mother and father put her on the train with her little brother Paul, her Grandma Joyce, and a small backpack filled with surprises. In the bag she knew there would be something to eat, something to drink, something to keep her warm, and at least one surprise she'd never even imagined...

As the train sat in the station, Janice pictured each stop it would make. She thought of all the friends who would get on and all the little animals that would watch it race across the valley and into the mountains.

She knew that the magic of Christmas Town was about to begin, just like always...

But tonight was a little different. Grandma wasn't here this year. A few weeks ago she had fallen down the front steps, and now she was recovering in a place that Janice couldn't even visit. As she thought about riding the train without Grandma, Janice felt a tear roll down her face. Mom and Dad had explained that Janice and Paul were old enough to make the trip to Christmas Town alone. It was exciting, but a little sad to be doing it without Grandma.

If only Grandma could be here, I wouldn't be so scared, thought Janice. She opened her bag, took out the sweater that Grandma had knitted for her, and wrapped herself in it for comfort. Then she decided to look deeper inside her bag and see what this year's surprise would be. There might be crayons, or a card game. Maybe a bag of candy. One year, she'd gotten a stuffed polar bear that looked just like her friend Bumblebee. Right at the top, she found the water bottle Dad had given her for her birthday last year. She took a sip and felt a little braver.

N ow the train was pulling out of the station, and the gentle rocking motion and the hum of the wheels on the track were already working their magic. She felt herself relax and begin to smile at everyone around her. Before she knew it, the conductor had announced the first stop, and Janice watched the children boarding the train with their families. "Sorry about your grandma," the conductor said as he punched Janice's ticket. "I heard she had a little accident."

Before she looked for her surprise, Janice decided to check on Paul. He was sitting up in the top of the dome car with his friend Mark, and they were already drinking hot chocolate and talking to the two little mice who'd gotten on at the first stop. Paul grinned at Janice, and his sparkling eyes told her that he was going to be all right.

ubble and Squeak, the two little gray field mice who rode the train with Paul every Christmas, were telling him all about the trouble they'd had with the farmer's new cat this fall. There were plenty of left-over kernels of corn for the mouse family, but that cat was making it harder and harder to get to the food.

Janice smiled at Bubble and Squeak and looked up in the overhead luggage rack to see if anyone was hiding up there yet. There were always a few small snowy owls who didn't understand that the Christmas train was a safe place for every creature. Maybe she'd look in her bag to see if there might be something she could share with them to make them a little less nervous. She opened her bag again and took out the gingerbread boy that Mom had baked yesterday. She carefully broke it into small pieces and left it for the frightened birds.

ust at that moment, Janice felt the train slowly come to a stop at the next station. She didn't have to look outside to know that the frozen pond would be shimmering on the other side of her window.

But of course she looked anyway, and as she did, her friend Wabash came careening on board the train. "Oh, my frozen tail fur," said the squirrel. "It's so good to see you all! I wasn't sure the train was coming this year, and it's so cold out there!" "Do you remember a year when this train didn't come?" squeaked Bubble. "It wouldn't seem like Christmas without a ride on this train! Some things never change." said Squeak.

But things had changed this year, at least for Janice. No one knew how scared she was to be riding the train without Grandma. *What if Grandma never gets to ride the train again? What if her legs don't heal and she can't even walk anymore?*

Janice clutched her little bag tightly and decided it was time to look inside for her surprise.

"Hello," said a little boy who had just boarded. "My name's Charlie. I've never ridden this train before. Is this your first time? Are you having fun? I am!" Janice put down her bag and made room for the little boy. She smiled at his excitement, forgetting how lonely she'd been feeling.

As the new passengers boarded, they were offered hot chocolate and ginger cookies. Everyone settled into their seats, and the train was off once more. Nibbling on her cookie and talking to the other children made her feel much better again.

It wasn't long before the conductor announced stop three... "Snowfort! Coming into Snowfort! Next stop, Snowfort." When the door opened, Janice could see a bright flash of white reflecting off the snow. And then with a gust of cold wind, in came a polar bear so large it didn't seem possible that he could fit through the door to the train. Bumblebee!

"**M**erry Christmas, everyone," said Bumblebee. "I'm so glad to see you all." Janice's heart warmed as he put two large paws around her. "But where's your grandma?" he asked Janice.

As Janice explained why Grandma couldn't be there this year, she felt her smile disappear. *Why does everyone have to keep asking about Grandma?* she said to herself. *Maybe it's time to look in my bag for that surprise.*

"I'm sorry to have made you sad," said Bumblebee, as he gave her another big bear hug. "But you've had some great trips with her, haven't you?" She snuggled next to him in the big double seat, as the train began to roll ahead. Once the train started moving, things always seemed better...

She picked up her bag and started to look inside, but just at that moment a large candy cane appeared. The elves were here! "Happy Christmas to you," they said together as she looked up. "How wonderful to see you this year! We were afraid you wouldn't make it."

As the elves told her all about the work they'd been doing getting ready for Christmas, Janice began to feel better again. But when they asked about her Grandma... "Now is the time," she said to the elves. "I need to see what's in my bag. It will help me stop thinking about Grandma."

But before she could open the bag, the conductor announced the stop at the old depot. Janice couldn't help smiling when she remembered all the times she'd visited her grandfather when he worked there. She looked out her window and thought of the little calico cat that always lived at the depot. In the summer, he watched for the train to go by from his favorite sunny spot beside the door. But at this time of the year, he wasn't always around.

As the passengers boarded the train, she thought she saw a streak of brown and white race past. *Yes!* In a few seconds, Zephyr was peering up at her from the back of the seat. "So good to see you, Janice! It's nice to be back on the train, isn't it? Merry Christmas."

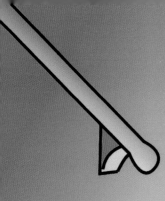hen the train stopped at Christmas Town, Janice watched Santa and a few more elves get on board the train. "He's coming!" shouted Paul, who was suddenly beside her. "Just like always!" *Just like always!* thought Janice, as she watched Santa make his way through the train.

With the train speeding down the tracks towards home, Janice wanted to open her bag, and she was surprised when she looked out the window and saw the lights of her town just ahead. *I'd better open this bag before we get home,* she thought.

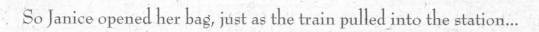So Janice opened her bag, just as the train pulled into the station...

In her bag, she found a small book filled with pictures of all the trips she'd taken on the Christmas Train with Grandma. At the back of the book were several blank pages with a note that said, "These pages are for today's trip and all the trips to come. Love, Grandma!"

You can count on me

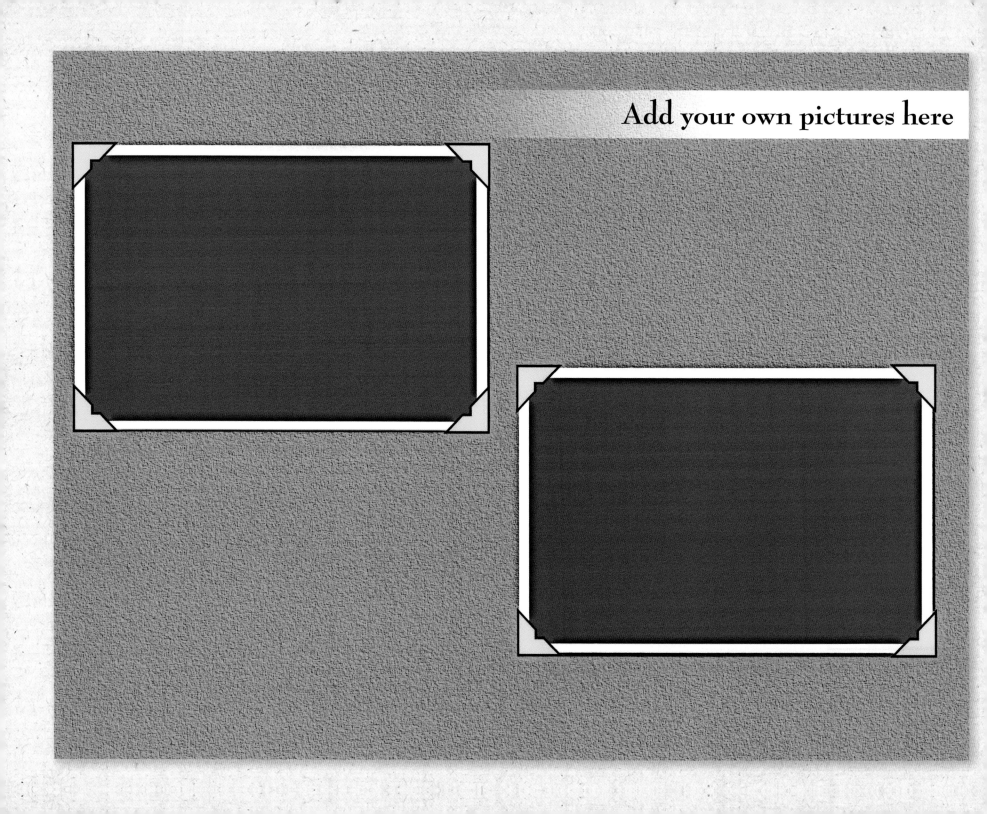

Add your own pictures here